Angelina Ballerina™

Angelina's First Day

Visit our website at:
www.autumnchildrensbooks.co.uk

Angelina leapt and twirled all around the kitchen. She was very excited!

"That big smile tells me you're feeling good about your first day at your new school," commented Mr. Mouseling.

"At Camembert Academy, I get to dance every day!" replied Angelina. "Let's go!"

Mr. Mouseling tried to keep up, but Angelina kept dancing ahead of him down the street.

"We're here!" Angelina announced as they turned a corner. She gazed up at her new school. Suddenly she was worried. "It's a lot bigger than my old school," she said quietly to herself.

As Angelina walked into the grand entrance hall, she began to feel even more nervous.

All of a sudden, two friendly mouselings bounded up to her.

"Welcome to Camembert! I'm Viki and this is Marco. You are going to be in our class."

Angelina felt better straight away. The mouselings were so kind and friendly!

Mr. Mouseling kissed her goodbye. “Have a great day,” he whispered in her ear.

Viki took Angelina's hand and introduced her to Gracie – another new friend!

Angelina's new friends then led her to the most amazing stage she had ever seen...

"We call this the Lunchtime Theatre," announced Marco.

"That's because anyone can perform up here when we are having our lunch," said Gracie as she struck a pose.

"Then when you finish your performance you get a red rose," explained Viki.

Angelina was excited to have a go, so she added her name to the list.

Soon it was time for Angelina's first dance lesson. She couldn't wait to practise ballet!

Before she could start, Marco began playing some very strange music on his violin. "Have you ever heard Celtic music before?" Marco asked.

“It is music that accompanies an Irish dance,” Viki said as she danced steps Angelina had never seen before.

Next, Marco began playing jazz music and Gracie moved and grooved. Angelina was beginning to wonder if she was going to fit in – all she knew was ballet.

Then, it was Angelina's turn to dance. She didn't want to just do ballet after seeing her new friends dance, so instead she tried something different. It was a bit of Viki's dance and a bit of Gracie's dance – at the same time!

"It's a bit hard to play the violin to that," Marco said.

"It's not your fault," Angelina sighed. "I don't know what I'm doing!"

She grabbed her bag and ran out of the room, feeling upset.

"This is the worst day of school ever!" Angelina cried as she buried her face in her hands.

Just then, Mrs. Mouseling and Polly arrived, carrying Angelina's lunch bag. "What is wrong, Angelina? Have you been crying?" Mrs. Mouseling asked.

“Nobody dances like I do!” Angelina wailed.

Polly showed her a picture she had drawn of Angelina doing ballet, but it didn’t make her feel any better. Angelina didn’t want to be different from the others in her class.

"Well, let's see," said Mrs. Mouseling. "Are you just like Polly? Or like me or your dad?"

"No..." Angelina replied.

"That's because everyone is different and that's okay," said Mrs. Mouseling.

Angelina suddenly understood. She tried to imagine what life would be like if everyone was the same and did exactly the same things. If everyone read the newspaper just like Dad or watered the plants just like Mum, it would be boring!

Angelina shuddered at the thought. “That would be horrible. Imagine only having one flavour of ice cream!”

“Or having exactly the same cheese pie every night,” Mrs. Mouseling agreed. Before leaving, Mrs. Mouseling gave Angelina a big hug and wished her luck for her performance.

That afternoon, it was time for the new students to perform in front of the whole school. Angelina took a deep breath and asked Marco to play some ballet music.

The music started and Angelina began to dance. She leapt and spun around the stage. The crowd clapped and cheered. Even her new teacher, Ms. Mimi, was impressed!

When Angelina finished her dance, Viki ran up on to the stage with a rose.

"You were so fantastic!" Viki cried. "Normally ballerinas are given a red rose, but we are giving you a yellow one because it is something new and different, just like you!"

"Wow, thanks," gasped Angelina. "It's great! Just like my new and different school."

It looked like Camembert Academy was just the right place for Angelina after all!